DIE WITH ME

D. L. DARBY

Help is Available

If you or anyone you know is in trouble and suffering
from abuse, the National Domestic Violence Hotline
is open 24/7
800-799-7233
https://www.thehotline.org/

CONTENT WARNING

Your mental health matters.
This book deals with very
heavy themes. For a list of
warnings, please visit my site.

Please read responsibly.

For Misty, who taught me things about myself I never knew

I loved you from the moment I saw you. Then you caused me the greatest pain I ever knew. I became your ghost and haunted you until you had no choice but to acknowledge me. By then it was too late.

I'd already become a demon.

D.L. DARBY

Drip.

Drip.

Drip.

The faucet in the seedy hotel I'm staying in—the ones where they rent the rooms by the hour—leaks steadily into the rusty, cracked porcelain of the sink.

Beyond the paper-thin walls, I can hear over-enthused grunts and moaning that sounds so rehearsed I wouldn't be surprised if they were shooting a porn film next door.

But this is the type of place where my monster won't think to look for me. The kind of establishment police stay away from, so I know I won't be bothered while I plan my next move.

Pain lances through my gut, pulsing in time with the needle piercing my skin. Pulling it taut, I tie off the last suture needed to sew my flesh back together.

Blood seeps from the cut, covering my fingertips, causing me to tighten my grip so the needle doesn't slip from my grasp.

My wound isn't fatal, just big enough to require stitches. Luca has a penchant for knives—or perhaps he favors them because they are my weapon of choice when I carve into another part of his delicious body.

When I warned my monster that I had found his hiding spot, I hadn't expected him to strike back so vigorously. I mean, I expected him to be pissed that I paralyzed him and left him on the floor of the strip club he's working at for someone to find—but I never expected to find myself caught up in our current game of cat and mouse.

Luca thinks he's the cat, but our score speaks for itself.

Misty - 3

Luca - 1

And what a thrilling game it's become.

The pink and blue lights from the hotel's large sign beam through the window, bathing the bed in a neon glow. Deciding not to close the curtains, I sit down and begin to remove the rest of my clothes. When I'm down to nothing but my bra and underwear, a tingling sensation blossoms along the back of my neck, slowly making its way down my spine.

My eyes snap to the window, searching the dark

night lit up by patches of vivid color. There's no one on the walkway or the stairs leading to the second floor. The parking lot is void of motion, with just a few empty vehicles in parking spots to the left or right of my room.

Yet, the feeling that someone is watching me grows with every second.

Is that you, il mio mostro? Have you found me?

The thought has my nipples puckering as the space between my legs comes alive with the idea of Luca out there, watching my every move.

I hate him. I've never hated someone as much as I hate the man who murdered my brother. But I'm also intrigued by him. He captured my attention when I was barely seventeen, and he's kept it ever since. For the last eight years, he's all I've been able to think about.

Oh, how sweet his blood will smell when I spill it. The way his head will tip back in pleasure as I ride his cock, catching him unawares in the throes of passion—his bronze eyes dimming as the life drains from them when I finally take my pound of flesh.

So why haven't you taken it yet?

Blocking out my inner thoughts, my eyes scan the lot again as I approach the glass. There's a patch of faded green on the far side, clotted with dusty, low bushes and short palms. Focusing on the spot directly across from my window, I catch the slightest movement.

It could be a palm leaf, blowing in the lazy, dry wind.

Or it could be my monster.

Keeping my eyes trained on the dark area, I reach up and unclasp the fastening of my bra. The cups spring free, straps slipping down my arms as I let the garment fall to the floor. My breasts hang full and heavy, nipples forming stiff peaks that point directly where I think I have an audience.

A glow appears in the dark—the cherry of a cigarette—followed by a billow of smoke that curls around the inky darkness.

My breath catches in my throat, a soft rasp as I trail my fingers down the swell of my breast and over one nipple, catching my nail on the tip before pinching it. My pussy is wet as the fingers of my other hand meet my opening. I stroke myself over the fabric of my underwear, more wetness gushing as the cherry burns brighter.

Releasing my nipple, I graze my fingers lightly over where Luca cut me earlier.

The figure steps forward. Just enough that the glow of the vacancy sign lights up his face right as my fingers swirl over my clit.

Raw need flows through me as Luca reveals himself.

Apparently, I didn't choose a good enough hiding place. But he isn't here to end our game.

He's here to watch a show.

I take a step back toward the bed. He takes one forward, sucking the end of his cigarette as though it's the very oxygen he needs to breathe.

My thighs hit the scratchy cotton of the comforter just as Luca approaches my window. There's a fading cut on his upper right cheek—compliments of me, of course. His thick cock is outlined against his jeans, hard and long. I sit, spreading my legs wide and pulling my thong to the side so he can see what a mess he's made me.

His eyes trail down my body before landing on my pussy. As though he couldn't care less that anyone could see him at any given time, he reaches down and undoes the button of his pants, pulling his dick out just enough to stroke it as he watches me.

I swirl my juices around my pussy lips before plunging two fingers inside, matching the pace he's set as he pumps his cock. My chest heaves, the angle of my body causing the wound on my lower abdomen to bleed through my amateur stitches; blood seeping down in small rivulets until it reaches my pussy.

"*Fuck,*" Luca mouths as he picks up his pace.

My teeth find my bottom lip, trying to keep a

keening moan from escaping my throat and failing miserably.

I want to know what it feels like to sink onto his cock.

I want to know what it feels like to have him fuck me so mercilessly that he'll make me bleed in an entirely different way.

I want to sink my blade into his flesh as he comes, mixing our fluids and forcing him to lick them off my lips so that a part of me can take root inside him before our lives end.

I fuck myself faster. Harder. My hips lift off the bed to meet my fingers, and I bury them inside me as far as they'll go. Blood begins to pour as I rip my stitches while stretching my body over the bed, throwing my head back, and crying my release to the water-stained ceiling.

White spots dot my vision as I breathe through wave after wave of intense, hot pleasure, lifting my head just in time to see Luca explode, white cum flowing through his fingers and spraying over the surface of my window.

His eyes harden, and his jaw tics.

Red creeps along the perimeter of my gaze as the pain sets in.

Looking down, I see that I've ripped nearly all my stitches out. Blood leaves trails down my mound and into the crevices of my slick flesh. As I sit up, my release gushes out of me, mixing with my red life substance.

Scooping it between two fingers, I rise from the bed and walk to where only the thin sheet of glass separates us; smearing it over where he came.

Luca's nostrils flare as he tucks himself away, watching as I paint him a message.

Fuck you.

He chuckles, and when he speaks, it's as if there's nothing between us at all. "I will, piccola demone. First, I'll fuck you. Then, I'll kill you."

Then he turns and walks away, back across the lot, before disappearing into the night.

Luca

An array of fragrances marries the thick scent of cigars, creating the heavily perfumed cloud I've come to associate with Vegas. Usually, the stench of fried food and sex accompany it, creating a nauseating combination that took months for me to figure out how to wash out of my clothes.

But this isn't that sort of establishment.

No, this strip club has more class than the ones my boss runs.

In a way, it reminds me of Désirer.

I stalk toward the back, where the private rooms are. The floral arrangement in my hands drips water from the flower cooler where I retrieved them, a gorgeous distraction that shields the lethal beauty within the bouquet.

She's called me here tonight. My piccola demone. *My little demon.*

And like a moth to a flame, I came. Unable to resist the temptation of drawing blood from her once more.

It's been like this for weeks now—this game of cat and mouse. We keep telling each other we will kill the other, but neither of us can deny the state of euphoria the other elicits.

If I'd known such a delicacy existed within Désirer's walls, I'd have moved on from Carmela in a heartbeat.

The woman I used to be so infatuated with would have never let me make her bleed. No, when Carmela captured my attention, I was forced to put my monster in a cage and lock the doors. She was my chance at a different life. A domestic one that I thought I wanted.

Now that Misty has come along and pried the bars open with a crowbar, I realize I could have never thoroughly tamed the beast within me.

"ID?" A man stops me outside the hall leading to the private rooms. Quietly, I hand my fake one over, unsure if Misty used it or my real name.

Apparently, it's the former, as the man hands it back over and checks off a name on his list. "She said you'd take care of the cameras?" he mentions as he holds out his hand.

Gruffly, I laugh. "Of course she did." *The little bitch.*

I deposit a few crisp hundreds in his hand before tucking my wallet back into the inner pocket of my suit jacket—right next to a syringe of Midazolam.

I don't want my little demon knocked out; just a little easier to handle while I take what I want from her tonight. I want her pliable. Willing. But unable to stab me in the back while she comes on my cock— which she would gladly do.

Our game doesn't end tonight.

The room is dripping in gold-colored embellishments from the faux-marbled flooring to the wall of liquid that runs horizontally through three of the walls, bubbling like there's actual champagne housed within the glass. A black leather booth encloses a small black-lacquered stage with a sparkling gold pole in the center of it.

And wrapped around the pole, wearing nothing but a flimsy thong, is my *piccola demone.*

"I was beginning to think you weren't going to show," she lilts as she wraps a leg around the glittering golden rod and uses her weight to spin upside down before righting herself again.

My cock hardens immediately as her full breasts bounce, nipples erect and just begging to be bitten. A rush of adrenaline courses through my veins when I see my handy work on her abdomen. A rugged slash of red puckered skin that's just now starting to fade back to the color of her flesh at the edges.

I step closer to the stage, imagining what it would feel like to pull her skin apart and watch the blood well at the surface. "We have to stop meeting like this. I'm beginning to think you truly enjoy my company. Not that you want to kill me, piccola demone."

She lets out the tinkling giggle that is her unique laugh. "There won't be many more meetings, il mio mostro. I'm growing tired of this game."

Something grips my chest, icy fingers of knobby bone crushing through the blackened organ. I place the roses on the leathery surface of the booth, gripping the edge of the stage to peer up at her. She flips upside down and spreads her legs wide.

The little slut is already soaked.

"You don't look tired. So fucking wet for me already," I growl.

Misty smirks, moving into a headstand position before gently, and expertly, kicking off the pole to lower her legs around my neck. Her body bends in half as she pushes her pussy in my face and undulates her hips, grinding against me.

Her juices soak my nose as I open my mouth to blow hot breath into her core. I wrap my hands around her thighs and hold her to me while I breathe her scent in—vanilla and roses and pure, unadulterated lust.

"I hate that you make me this way," she whispers from her contorted position.

"No, you don't," I speak directly into her, shoving her thong into her hole with my nose before I lick a path up her slit. I moan, loud and disgustingly, as I sloppily kiss her clit. "If you truly hated it, you'd never have sought me out again."

She exhales a sharp breath as my teeth close over her sensitive bundle of nerves, nibbling on her hard enough to make her hips buck. Her skin pulls taut between my teeth as she retreats. I make her work for it, tightening my bite before finally letting go when she squeals.

With her eyebrows furrowed deeply and her seafoam orbs shining bright with rage, she snarls, "Make no mistake, il mio mostro. I'll be your end. *That* is the only reason I found you again."

"And I'll be yours, piccola demone," I say darkly.

She snorts and goes to move off the stage, opening those sinful lips to retort when I reach into my jacket and pull the syringe out, stabbing her in the thigh quickly. The dosage I give her is so low it will take a while to kick in—which is fine because I want to take my time with her tonight.

Growling like a feral cat, she launches herself at me after knocking the needle away. Long, black-painted nails pierce my cheeks as she scratches at me, keening like an animal in heat as she attacks my throat with her teeth and bites down like she's trying to rip out my jugular.

Twisting her long, chestnut waves in my hand, I pull her off me with a roar before dragging her from the stage. She scrambles to regain her footing, hands continuing to claw at me with frenzied, uncalculated blows.

"It seems that you're not on your A game tonight." I chuckle, tossing her to the floor. I remove my jacket and quickly make work of the buttons on my shirt before pulling it over my head.

Misty glares up at me from the floor, making no effort to get up. Her eyes rake over my muscles as my hands move to my belt. "Who's to say I don't have something up my sleeve for later?"

A crack resonates through the room as I swiftly pull my belt from its loops and whip it out. "You're already naked," I bend down to grab ahold of the material covering her between her legs and rip it away from her body, baring the rest of her to me, "so unless you have something hiding in that pretty little cunt, I'll take my chances."

Dropping to my knees, I knock her back with my

sheer size, reaching down to shove two fingers inside of her. She's warm and tight and so goddamn wet that I groan. "Look at that. Nothing here. Completely empty and ready for my cock to destroy."

She laughs; the melodic, tinkling giggle filling the room as her nails find purchase in my shoulders and drag down my arms. I swallow the sound as our lips battle. Her legs cage my hips, the lurid sounds of her pussy devouring my fingers taking its place as her tight walls suction around my digits, pulsating with a life of its own.

My cock throbs. So fucking ready to be consumed by her heat. But it's not time yet.

Tearing myself away from her, I smirk at the whimper of outrage that leaves her lips. She tries to rise, but her movements are sluggish. She writhes on the floor as she watches me reach for the roses, eyes widening with intrigue as I pull a slim knife from the bouquet.

"Coward," the word is slow as it leaves her lips.

"Oh, I'm not going to kill you tonight," I explain, wrapping my free hand around her hair to drag her to a sitting position. I'm too tall, and it's not the right height for what I want to do to her, so I pick her up and hoist her over my shoulder, bringing her over to where the booth flattens like a chaise. "Tonight, I'm going to leave you wanting while I even the score between us."

She makes an unintelligible sound as I slam her down on the leather cushions before propping her up. I set the knife on the stage, quickly ridding myself of my pants. Her tongue darts out to wet her lips as she eyes my throbbing length. There's already precum beaded at the tip of my flushed crown as I grab my cock in one hand and the knife in the other.

Kneeling on the leather, I smear it over her mouth as I bring the blade to her neck. "Open your mouth and show me how much you hate me. And don't you even think about trying to bite it off, or I'll end your life before you can finish the job."

A gasp flies from her lips as I press the edge of the blade into her skin hard enough that a thin line of blood wells at the surface. I take the opportunity to shove my cock between her open lips, thrusting in nearly to my root.

Misty's head bobs automatically, adjusting to take my size, seafoam glazing over with lust as she moans around me. She sucks hard as I retreat as if trying to stop me from leaving the heat of her willing mouth. I pull out all the way, watching as she licks and sucks the tip before gathering the saliva in her mouth and letting it pool as I shove my way back inside. Her head hits the back of the booth as I take over her throat.

She tries to swallow around me, her throat constricting to trap my dick in a vise grip for a second that has me tipping my head back in pleasure. "Fuck, why couldn't you have approached me sooner?"

As I look back down, our eyes lock as she slowly raises her hands to lay her palms against my thighs. I tangle my hand in her strands again, tightening my fingers to hold her head down on me. "Think of all the fun we could have had at Désirer."

There's a sharp prick as she begins to struggle, but I refuse to let her go and press the knife into her flesh in a different place, drawing blood as she pushes against me. After a few more moments, I release her, pulling out of her mouth completely.

Her chest heaves as she gasps for air, drawing my attention to her rosy nipples. Unhurriedly, I drag the knife along her skin, down past her collarbone, and over the swell of her breast before I press the tip into the hardened peak. Without a word, she looks down to watch as I circle her areola, blood following the trail I make.

"What do you have to say for yourself, Misty? Why'd you wait so long to find me?"

She opens her mouth to answer, and I shove my cock back between her lips, cutting off her words and forcing them into a jumble of incoherent syllables. But instead of getting angry, she closes her eyes and sucks my cock like her life depends on it, even though I've assured her that, for tonight, it doesn't.

Dragging the knife upward again, I enjoy the goosebumps that erupt over her skin. My fingers tighten as I steel myself from going too deep. Her teeth graze my length with every cut I make until the left side of her is bloody from her breast to her neck.

"So fucking beautiful." Palming the knife, I hold her head to me as I pull her up, making her scramble onto her shins. I swipe two fingers through her blood and hold them up for her to see. "I've got your saliva on my dick, your blood on my hands, and your pussy juices leaking all over the booth. Tell me, Misty, do you want to come? Does this turn you on as much as it does me?"

Tears line her eyes as she struggles to breathe, and my cock jumps in her throat at the sight. I let her go and push her away, giving her a moment of reprieve as she slumps back. A trail of saliva falls from her lips, connecting to my cock as it falls from her mouth and bobs in the air between us.

"Tell me what you want, piccola demone. Do you want to ride my face until that euphoric orgasm hits? Do you want me to fuck you rough and hard until you're bleeding? Tell me."

Her legs fall open, her pussy pink and flushed and so wet she might have already come. Her clit is engorged, peeking up at me from under the hood, just begging for me to pay attention to it.

She moans as I lay the flat of the blade directly

over her wet flesh, hips rising to meet the bloodied metal. "Yes," she whispers, sliding down until she's lying on her back, hips undulating lazily against the knife. "Yes to it all."

"Sick fucking slut," I laugh the words into the air like a prayer. This is the type of religion I'm into. And my piccola demone is the most perfect goddess I've ever worshiped.

"Ahh!" she lets out a cry as the tip of the knife pokes her hood. A thick, creamy stream releases from her pussy as it tightens around the air. She watches as I scoop it with my bloodied fingers and stick them in my mouth, making a show of licking them clean.

Her bottom lip disappears between her teeth, her entire lower face glistening with saliva and my precum. "How does it taste?" She sounds so fucking innocent when she asks. So eager to hear me tell her it's the best damn thing I've ever tasted.

"Like poison," I tell her before slamming my cock into her so hard it rocks her body backward. I lay the knife above her head before gathering her wrists in one hand to make sure she can't go after it.

Every thrust is rough. Her tits bounce. Her head thrashes back and forth. A sultry smile parts her lips as she stares up at me reverently because she thinks she's getting exactly what she wants.

Sweat begins to bead at my hairline as I pound into her, our flesh slapping together as her arousal mixes with the blood that's pooling from the cut I made just above her clit. My sweat smears the blood from every cut as I lean down and bury my face in her neck. My saliva blends with it as I clamp my teeth around a mouthful of flesh and bite down as I drill my cock so deep into her she's going to feel my cum coat the insides of her chest.

Her breathing picks up, her body shifting to press her clit against my pubic bone for friction, but I angle my hips in a way where I fuck her deeper, and she gets nothing more than the rock-hard length of my dick. That's it.

Jackhammering my hips and relishing in her squeals, I come hard and continue biting her through it, spilling hot, thick ropes of cum along her slick walls before pulling out to empty the rest onto her body. I paint her pussy, her stomach, and her tits before finishing on her face.

And she doesn't come at all.

She's a goddamn masterpiece when I'm finally spent. Covered in blood and cum, and dripping with so much ire that she's probably imagining me burning to ashes right now.

I release her wrists and grab the knife before moving off the booth to gather my clothes.

Misty is more than likely in the height of her drugged state. Heavy with a semi-state of sedation and unable to come after me.

"Pretty sure this evens the score, piccola demone."

The only answer I get is silence as I dress and leave her, much like she left me when she began our game.

Misty

Before him, I was an innocent, sweet little girl who wanted to make her brother proud by becoming a doctor.

After him, I became the demon he's so aptly named me. Once he took my brother away and destroyed any chance I had at a future.

"You still don't know me, do you?" I arch my back, whispering into his ear as I lay my head back on his shoulder and grind against his hard cock.

Tonight, we have a non-verbal truce. I'm still healing from our last game, and neither of us wishes to end things just yet, so we agreed to meet somewhere we can't hide. Somewhere we can still have fun, just without our knives.

The strip club is neutral and high-end and enforces a strict dress code. A plush red velvet rope secures our area from the outside riff-raff yet puts us on display for whoever wishes to observe.

To everyone here, we're just a couple of fucked up individuals who like to be watched.

Luca's left hand cradles his crystal tumbler of whiskey as it rests on the arm of the crushed velvet armchair we're sitting in. His right hand winds around my waist, curling to pull me closer before dipping lower to find the slit in my see-through dress.

His fingers swipe between my pussy lips, lazily playing with my clit as he widens his legs and pushes his hips up into my ass. I can feel the outline of his length as he rubs it against me, every nerve ending firing off with warm sparks. "I've thought long and hard about where we might have met before. I'd like to think I could never forget those eyes."

"Yet, you did," I state flatly. Pushing off him, I stand. He lets me go, eyes dragging down my body as I turn to look at him. His gaze makes me feel so alive, even when I know it's the last thing I'll see before death.

I take his tumbler, the large round ice cube clinking against the glass as I raise it to my lips and swallow the remaining amber liquid, welcoming the smoky trail that burns as it slides down my throat.

Holding Luca's stare, I walk to the edge of the

rope, handing the glass to our personal attendant, who is six feet of solid, oiled muscle and all too eager to please. "Fetch us a refill," I command.

This persona is so far from the woman I used to be. Sometimes, it's jarring how rude, how vile, how *demonic* I've become—the perfect little demon for her perfect big, bad monster.

"Perhaps when I return," the waiter takes the glass in one hand then lifts my knuckles to his lips, "you'd like an extra mouth on this gorgeous body."

"Perhaps you'd like your tongue cut from your inappropriate mouth." Luca's words charge the air with warning.

"Oh, but this is the poor man's job—to ensure we're completely taken care of. If he's asking if I need an extra mouth, it must be because I don't look satisfied," I tease seductively, turning to wink at the man who pays Luca no mind.

Bad decision, my darling. Il mio mostro is not a creature to ignore.

As the man walks away, Luca crooks a finger in my direction as he stands. "Sit."

I approach him, taking my time as every slow sway of my hips grinds on his nerves. When we are chest to chest, I tilt my head back to look at him but don't take his place on the chair. His jaw tics, nostrils flaring as my lace-covered nipples brush against his bare chest where his shirt is unbuttoned.

Luca has always been able to turn me on with a simple glance. The first time I laid eyes on him, I fell in love. Back when I was a stupid, naïve girl.

Now, I wonder how different things might have been if he'd just paid me a sliver of the attention I have now.

Our chests heave. Control is a tangible thing between us that we both have hold of—like a stick of dynamite that burns at both ends, yet neither of us relinquishes even though we'll both be caught in the blast.

He grips my biceps, his touch sending sparks of electricity through my flesh as he guides me to the chair, our eyes never disconnecting. Luca reaches for the lace fabric of my dress and fists it, slowly tearing the see-through material. "You may be a creature of the underworld, piccola demone. But you are *my* creature, do you hear me? *Mine* to satisfy, *mine* to withhold pleasure from, *mine* to torture. You are mine to do with what I please, and I will kill anyone else who dares to even think of touching you."

With every word, he punctuates his meaning with another rip until I'm bare before him. I can feel more than just his eyes on me—on us. But I dare not look away from my monster. There's a fire in his eyes that burns only for me. A fire I set. A reminder that this could have been mine long ago if I'd just made my move sooner instead of waiting to exact my revenge.

A foreshadowing of my future.

For when I kill Luca, I will follow him to the depths of Hell because for as much as I am his, he will forever be mine.

"Every person in here is thinking of touching me right now." I smirk, leaning back against the crushed velvet, my black Louboutins clicking against the floor as I spread my legs wide one at a time. "What will you do, il mio mostro? Will you cut out all of their eyes? Or will you show them who I belong to?"

His eyes rove the cuts that are still healing on the left side of my body, taking in his handiwork from the bite mark that's still bruised to the puffy skin of my hood, where he pierced me with his knife.

I'm fully prepared for Luca to force me to choke on his cock again. Though I was drugged, I enjoyed the way he handled me. His cock is perfect—long and thick and veiny—and I've dreamt about wrapping my lips around it once more and biting down as he spills down my throat.

I'm surprised, however, when he slowly bends his knees to kneel before me.

He chuckles as my eyes widen a fraction. His hands cup beneath my thighs, raising my legs to rest over his shoulders. "Tonight, I will show them all what only I can do to you. Because even if there were someone else between your thighs, it's me you would be thinking of."

"Fuck you, Luca." I spit the words as he lowers his head to lick between my lower lips. My abdomen clenches, pure molten desire flowing up my spine and spilling down my legs.

I tense, heels digging into his back as he draws my flesh into his mouth, gently laving my wound with the flat of his tongue before he replies, "You did, Misty. Or rather, I fucked you."

He kisses my clit. "And I'll do it again."

Another kiss. "And again."

Another. "And again."

The velvet is smooth beneath my hands as I clutch the back of the chair, head tipped back as he slowly devours me. Luca doesn't just eat my pussy, he savors it like he's on death row, and I'm his last meal—consuming me with the kind of patience only a dead man walking would have.

"Open your eyes and watch me," he commands from between my legs.

His words cut my building release off, and a whine escapes my chest as I do what he says because I desperately want to come. I want to launch myself at him and ride his beautiful face until my juices become part of his new skincare routine. I want my essence to be the only thing he drinks—the only nectar he needs to survive.

His lips rise and fall as he sucks my clit the way he would a candy that he's trying to get to the liquid center of. His deep brown eyes lock on mine, changing his pace when he reads in them that something isn't working, focusing on what does when my lids drop halfway, and I struggle to keep my eyes from rolling to the back of my head.

Luca's tongue strokes and licks, and his lips suck and tease as he works my flesh to his will and my pleasure. And when I come, he swallows me down as though he's afraid to spill a single drop.

"Fuck! Yes. Please," falls from my lips in a string of repeated jumbled words as he continues to eat me like a man starved.

He lets out a grunt as my fingers twist in his hair, pulling tightly as I attempt to fuse his lips to my pussy. Every muscle is tense, every single cell on fire. My breasts heave with labored breaths, my mouth opening in a silent scream that cuts off my airway. A hot, burning ball tightly coils in my abdomen before snapping and shooting downward, flowing through me and into Luca's mouth as he moans in approval.

Using his hair, I try to yank him away, bending in half to use my weight as leverage, but he uses it to his advantage. Never letting me go, he grips my thighs harder, scooping his arms beneath me and rising with my legs wrapped around his head, his mouth still glued between my thighs.

"Luca, please," I sob as he stands, turning to sit in the chair. He lowers himself, maneuvering me to slide down his body, lips kissing every inch of me until I'm straddling his lap and we're nose to nose.

His arms are warm as they wrap around me, shielding my nakedness from the crowd that gathered around our private area. We breathe heavily into the space between us, neither having anything to say as the act that just occurred settles itself, louder in this particular moment than words could ever be.

Luca brought me pleasure, not pain—*willingly*—just to show those watching what he could reduce me to. Not to humiliate me, but to assert ownership.

I knew this, and still, I let it happen.

Confusion dances with lust in both our eyes. Neither of us sated, yet both unsure of how to proceed.

Slowly, as if we're both magnets, our heads draw closer together, canting to opposite sides, burnished bronze meeting cool seafoam as our lips touch.

It isn't like it is in a romantic movie. We don't lose ourselves in the kiss. Our mouths mold together, and I watch him warily while tasting myself on his flesh. And he watches me just the same, as if I'd take the opportunity to gouge out his eyes the moment he closes them.

But then, in a moment of pure lunacy, I melt against him, opening my mouth to claim his in a searing kiss that has my eyes fluttering closed.

Only to see my dead brother glaring at me through the darkness.

I pull back with a jolt, snapping open my lids just in time to see his eyes widen as well—meaning that as soon as I let myself be vulnerable, he did the same.

"I need…I need to go to the bathroom…to clean up." The words taste like ash in my mouth as I scramble off his lap.

Without a word, he lifts his arms and tears his shirt from his shoulders, pulling it down over me to cover my body like a minidress. The crowd parts as I make my way to the bathroom not far from where we're set up. No one dares approach me. And when I make it to the door, I turn back to see that Luca is watching me walk away from him, puzzlement etched into his already chiseled features.

The water is cold when I splash it onto my face, regarding my reflection in the mirror. "Get it together," I whisper. "Now isn't the time to catch feelings for him again."

As I turn to leave, a man's voice rings out, unmistakable as it echoes throughout the room. *"It was never the time. Yet that didn't stop you, did it?"*

Whirling around, I see a clear image of my brother, Adam, in the mirror behind me. He looks handsome, blue-green eyes shining, skin clear of the blood I last saw smeared on it, wearing the new suit he had on the day he died—compliments of the Morroni family.

Checking over my shoulder, I see the room is empty except for me.

"You're supposed to avenge me. Not be his whore!" he spits out nastily, tone so full of disgust that I drop my eyes to the counter.

"I know," I tell him softly. "I know."

When my eyes lift again, he's gone, just like I know he will be.

Just like I know, he's never truly there.

Misty

"Marisela, I need you to stop arguing with me. I'll only be gone a few hours. Keep your head down and stay out of trouble. I'll be back before you know it." My brother adjusts his tie for the fourth time in the last few minutes, making it even more crooked than it was before.

I knock his hands away and step in front of him, drawing his eyes from his reflection in the mirror as I redo his simple knot. "Adam, this isn't funny. Getting involved with the mob isn't going to solve our problems!"

"Neither is sticking around here, Mari. If I don't start making some money soon, we're gonna be on the streets. It's bad enough your counselor has been poking around. You're barely seventeen. They can take you and put you in the system for a year. Is that what you want?" he asks. His tone is full of exasperation, words quavering with hopeless anger at our situation.

For as long as I can remember, it's been Adam and me against the world. Our parents were drug addicts who didn't give a shit about us, let alone about giving us a better life. Thanks to Adam managing to find us food and clothes, we've always scraped by without raising too much suspicion about our living conditions.

The system would have no doubt separated us. And my brother, the best man I'll ever know, has always made sure that never happened. No matter the lengths he's had to go through to ensure we always have what we need.

"No," I say quietly, finishing his knot and adjusting his collar. "I just wish you'd let me help. I can get a job and—"

"We've talked about this, Mari. I want you to focus on school." He cups my cheeks, leaning his forehead on mine as our matching blue-green gazes lock. "Focus on getting as many scholarships as you can. You're going to get out of this place and become a big hot-shot doctor someday."

His words twist and tighten my intestines. There's so much pressure to have a better future, when I could be helping us now.

As his hands fall away, my gaze journeys down the length of his navy Kiton suit that could pay for at least three months' worth of our rent. "How did you even get involved with the Morronis, Adam?"

My brother checks his watch, a knock-off Rolex that looks like it's seen better days up close but looks expensive from far away. "The less you know, the better. He's going to be here any second. You should go to your room. Don't you have homework or something you should be doing?"

His nerves are frazzled, and the telltale signs of stress are beginning to show on his features. Sweat beads at his hairline, and his eyes keep bouncing from me to the door to his watch.

"I want to know who you're leaving with, Adam. I don't like this. Why would they even employ you? You're young and know nothing about their world. I'm sorry to say this, but you're not exactly bodyguard material," I jest, my tone a little lighter as I reach out and pinch his skinny arm. He looks like he's days from wasting away, always making sure there's enough food for me—even if that means he goes without a meal for a day or two.

He laughs. It's hollow and short-lived as a knock interrupts whatever he's about to say in return.

"Marisela, go. Now," he pleads.

But I'm already halfway to the door, pulling it open before Adam can stop me.

It feels like time stops as a set of burnished bronze eyes fall from a frame well over six feet tall—tan, olive skin, a head of thick, dark hair, and the most chiseled jawline I've ever seen make up the man standing on the other side of the threshold.

"Well, well. Look at those beautiful eyes—misty, like the sea at dawn." The man chuckles as he leans against the doorframe and drags his eyes down the length of my body. I feel like a fly who's just been caught in a spider's web.

A very gorgeous spider, who looks like a mythological deity.

Dumbstruck by his ethereal beauty, my mouth opens and closes like a fish out of water before I stupidly reply, "Do you like the sea?" My brows furrow as I realize how dopey I sound, white knuckling the door like it's a lifeline.

He winks, and my insides flutter like a thousand butterflies have just escaped their cocoons and are shaking their newly formed wings for the first time. "In another life, it would have been my greatest love."

I want to be your greatest love. *The thought flickers through my mind, voiceless. I'm only a teenager. I've never been in love. I've never even had a boyfriend. But this man —this God—whoever he is, I want to be his everything.*

I want to ask him if he knows my name literally means 'star of the sea', but the softness his eyes hold for me hardens as he looks over Adam in the suit. "Acceptable." His voice is rougher when he speaks this time—booming into the small space of our one-bedroom apartment and echoing off the bare walls. "Ready to go?"

Adam's footsteps approach from behind, and though I don't want to pull my eyes from the man before me, as my brother's hand finds the small of my back, my head whips to the side to see a look of disapproval stretched across his face. "Lock the door behind us. Don't let anyone in while I'm gone. If Howie comes by hollering about the rent, pretend like you aren't home. Do you understand?"

I nod sheepishly, cheeks growing warm as Adam speaks

to me as though I'm a small child. My eyes flit back to the man taking up the entire space of the doorframe. His muscles ripple beneath his button-down shirt, threatening to tear the fabric beneath his suit jacket, as he pulls out his phone.

"Take care of my brother." I try to sound threatening. He laughs in return, fingers flying over the screen without paying me any attention other than his uncaring chuckle.

"Can I have a second with my sister, Luca? Please?"

Luca.

Of course, his name is just as sexy as he is.

Luca makes a sound that lands somewhere between a grunt and a huff before turning and leaving without another word. I watch him go, very nearly calling out after him.

Adam's fingers wrap around my bicep, and only then do I realize I'm halfway over the threshold in pursuit of Luca. My foot hits the floor with a defeated thud, and I allow my brother to pull me back into our tiny apartment.

"Don't even think about it, Mari." His warning is sharp as his fingers dig into my skin. "I don't want you getting caught up in this."

"I don't want you caught up in it either, Adam. Everyone knows how dangerous the Morronis are. For all you know, you could be walking into a room where they don't expect you to make it out alive! And they won't care! You mean nothing to them!" I rip my arm from his grasp and launch myself into his arms, hugging his waist. "You mean everything to me. You're all I have. Maybe…maybe I could—"

"Don't even finish that sentence. You're my little sister. It's my job to take care of you, not the other way around." He squeezes me tightly before gently pushing me away.

"Everyone knows how easy it is for a woman to make money these days. If I can make myself invaluable—"

"Stop! Mari, just stop. Please. We're just talking in circles, and I have to go. I'll be back later tonight, okay? Do your homework. And get those dark thoughts out of your pretty little head." He knocks his knuckles against my forehead before heading out the door. "You're not going to sell yourself. Over my cold, dead body."

Luca

"The next time I saw him, he was covered in blood. He managed to escape wherever you guys were and make it home mere seconds before he died. The last words on his lips were that he was sorry and that it was you who shot him." Misty spits her words as though they taste like garbage. "I ended up selling my body just to survive. I never did make it to medical school."

As she tells her tale of tragedy, I recall that night her brother died. He was just a kid looking to make a quick buck. I felt sorry for him, and would never have hired him for any type of job. He was too young. Too inexperienced.

But my father had been impressed with how the weedy twirp had walked into our restaurant and promised to pledge his allegiance to the Morroni name. I didn't know what he needed the money for, but after picking him up at his shoebox apartment, I assumed it was to take better care of his little sister.

I'm not ashamed to say he meant nothing to me— that I didn't care if he caught the stray bullet meant for a member of a rival family we met that night. I didn't stop to look for him when the shootout was over. I didn't bother seeing if he was still alive or dead. He never crossed my mind as I reported the evening's events to my father.

And I never thought of Misty again after that night.

But fuck if I'm going to tell her that *now*.

It would make no difference, other than to anger her further. And my piccola demone is pissed off enough as it is.

Blood drips steadily from the cut at my temple— compliments of Misty's wineglass—when she walked behind me to *admire the view* of the city from my living room windows.

I don't know why I asked her to my apartment tonight.

It's clear that after our last meeting, she wants me dead now, more than ever.

But it's also clear that Misty can't keep her hands off me. Nor I her. We can't stop fucking and carving each other up long enough to land a truly lethal blow.

The tip of the curved blade she holds pierces my

inner thigh, just enough to draw blood as she drags it up toward my cock, which is rock hard and dripping with precum. My wrists ache as I try again to snap the rope that ties them together behind my chair.

Whatever the fuck she used is scratching my skin raw and won't break, no matter how much force I put into pulling my hands apart. She's tied my ankles as well, but even though they're not bound as tightly, there's no getting out of my restraints.

"I'm sorry about your brother," I hiss through my clenched teeth.

"No, you're not," she croons. Her palm is slippery as she wraps it around my shaft, covered in blood from a cut she made over my left pec. My chest tightens, eyes growing wide in alarm as she places the curve of the blade around my dick and smiles. "I could end your life like this, you know. One swift slice and I could remove your most cherished organ and let you bleed out while you watch me burn it to ash."

Regardless of the danger it's in, my cock jumps in her hand as though it's up for its own castration. "You won't." I swallow the curse that sits in my throat like a weighted ball of lead. "You love that part of me too much."

Quicker than I can track, she flings the blade away from us and sinks onto me. Her pussy is already wet as it devours every inch of my length, warm and inviting as she molds around me like we were made for each other.

Her nipples trace the blood on my chest, painting a masterpiece as she rocks against me. Her skin is slick with the combination of my blood and our sweat. My clothes are tattered and torn around my chair, ruined by her blade once she finished tying my hands together and binding my feet to the legs of the dining room chair.

"God, I hate it so fucking much that you're right." She lifts up and sinks back down slowly. I can't help but watch where we're joined, fascinated with the way her pussy lips spread around my flushed crown and greedily suck my cock.

I can feel her flexing her inner walls as she seats herself fully on my lap and stops moving. Her lips stretch over her whitened teeth as she plays with the hair at my nape. I flex my dick in return, making it jump inside her and tap her upper wall.

"You don't hate it," I mock as I buck my hips the best I can in our current position. "You love every second of it. And you hate yourself for it. You hate yourself for being such a fucking slut for your brother's murderer, don't you?" I buck again more forcefully, picking up pace as I bounce her on my lap, pushing the soles of my feet against the floor for leverage.

The sting of her hand across my face bites my

cheeks twice before she grips them with her nails so hard I know I'll have marks. Anger burns brightly in her irises, lighting up her eyes like a stormy Caribbean Sea. "I hate you, Luca. I may love your cock, but make no mistake. I. Hate. *You.*"

Trying to prove a point, her teeth find my bottom lip as she snarls a kiss into my lips. Our tongues battle, teeth nipping as she pulls my hair and grinds against me, chasing an orgasm we both want while also never wanting this moment to end.

Even with my hands and feet bound, Misty continues to find new ways to make me feel *alive.* For ways to satiate the beast within me, yet come out the other side still standing. Still breathing.

Still yearning to capture this hellish creature and make her come over and over for all of eternity.

Lust, gluttony, greed, and wrath all roll into a bloody cloud of ecstasy as her mouth opens, and she cries her release into the air, spilling all over my lap.

And still, I want more.

I lean forward and capture her lower lip between my teeth and bite down, drawing her life substance as I fuck her through another orgasm. She screams into my mouth as her blood spills down our chins, her nails scraping at my face. The chair creaks beneath us, our weight daring the wood to give out as she rides me like she would a bronco at a rodeo.

I release her with a roar as I fill her full of rope

after hot rope of my cum, splashing against her walls, painting her as mine. "Hate me all you want, piccola demone. You fuck better when you're angry."

A frown mars her beautiful face as she wipes the blood away with her fingers and shoves them in my mouth, pulling them back out before I can bite down. The taste of her—sweet and coppery—mingles between our mouths as she pushes her lips to mine. Her tongue slides along my teeth before mine joins in the bloody dance.

As we kiss, her hands slide behind the chair, down to where my wrists are bloody and raw from rubbing against the scratchy rope. She moves like she's going to untie me, but then pauses, drawing back and climbing off my lap.

"Untie me, Misty," I command softly. Gentler than I've ever spoken to her before.

A thick glob of our combined cum spills from between her legs, dripping down her thighs as she laughs. She's a work of art that already has my cock hardening again—insatiable when it comes to this woman.

Her eyes snap over my shoulder, glazing over for a moment before they refocus, and she looks down at me again. "No. No, I don't think I will."

Warning bells go off in my head. Leaving me paralyzed in the strip club was one thing. Someone was sure to find me eventually, or the paralytic would have worn off.

But no one knows where I live except Giuseppe and my father.

"Misty." Her name is sharp and urgent on my tongue.

Her eyes narrow as she reaches between her legs to scoop up our mess. She swipes her fingers through the blood on my chest and holds them up to my lips. "Taste how sweet we are together, il mio mostro."

My mouth opens on its own accord, lips wrapping around the pads and sucking our tangy, metallic mixture off her fingers. Her cheeks flush pink as she watches my mouth, lips parting in an O that I know has her pussy wet again.

"Untie me, Misty," I repeat when I finish. "And I'll taste how sweet we are together from between your thighs."

"I don't know, I rather like having you at my mercy," she lilts as she steps slowly around the chair, dragging her fingers from my mouth to my neck, over my shoulder, and down my arm to slide her palm into mine. "I used to dream about what these hands could do to me. I knew it was wrong to fantasize about the very hands that killed Adam, but that's what made selling myself so much more bearable—imagining that you were the one touching me. Thinking about all the ways you could make me feel good. Wondering if you'd take your time, or steal my pleasure quickly."

Her fingers dance along the marks on my skin from the rope, the edge of her nails digging into the raw flesh. "But you never noticed me. Not then. Not when I arrived at Désirer. Not when I stood right in front of you and asked if you wanted to fuck. You didn't even recognize the misty-eyed girl you once told had beautiful eyes."

"I met you *once*, Misty. In passing," I growl as she digs her nails in harder.

She continues, ignoring my pain. "It's why I picked the name Misty, you know. When you told me the sea would have been your greatest love in another life, I followed you into that next life. I watched silently—waited *patiently* to become that great love so I could hurt you in the worst way imaginable. Just like you hurt me. I was employed at Désirer long before you even realized it. It was over a year before you finally *looked* at me."

"At Désirer I was–"

"In love with Carmela, I know." Her tone goes flat and takes on a hint of aggravation. The sounds of her walking away and getting redressed accompany her following words. "I studied her for a long time, trying to figure out what it was about her that kept you so enraptured. Anyone could have told you how *that* would end. It was never going to be you, yet you still worshiped the ground she walked on."

"You sound jealous." I know I shouldn't irritate her further than she already is at the mention of the woman I used to be in love with—or at least thought I was in love with—but there's something deep inside me that loves hearing the jealousy seeping into her cadence.

A carnal hunger with the need to fuel her fire.

Her stilettos on the hardwood are loud as she reappears in my vision, fully dressed and flipping the top to a lighter. "I used to be, Luca. But look at where loving her got you." She gestures down my body with a smirk. "Now, you're just a pathetic man. Waiting in the shadows until I take pity on you and finally end your life."

I reel at her sudden change in demeanor. Misty's no longer playful. No longer full of red-hot rage and desire. She's upset, and it's plain as day on her face. It sparks something else in my chest. Something I didn't even know I was capable of feeling—a long-lost tenderness that tries to burrow its way out.

That wants to protect her—even if it's me she needs protecting from.

"Misty, I—"

"We could have been so good together. If you hadn't murdered my broth—"

"I didn't murder him, Misty. He got caught in the

crossfire." My admission has her eyes growing wide before they fill with outrage.

"Liar!" she screams so harshly that her entire body shakes. So loudly that my bones rattle in my very chest. "And if that *were* the truth, why didn't you come back for me?!"

I struggle with the choice that lies before me. Do I tell her I didn't care then, but I do now? Do I say nothing? Will my silence be worse than the truth?

Will she even believe that my feelings have changed? Will she believe her monster has a heart that now beats only for her?

"Does it matter what I did or didn't do back then when it comes to you, *piccola demone*? We're together now. I didn't murder your brother, so your revenge plan is meaningless. You're trying to avenge someone who happened to be in the wrong place at the wrong time. I would have never given him a second glance had he not stormed in and convinced my father to give him a chance."

Her head swings to the side, appraising the air as if someone is talking to her, but there's no one there. "You're lying," she murmurs. It's quiet, with an uptick at the end, like she's asking a question but isn't entirely sure she wants to.

"I'm not. I didn't come for you that night because that moment was insignificant to me," I tell her honestly, watching her bristle at my words. "If I knew then what I know now, I'd have gone back for you. I'd have protected you."

I don't tell her that it wouldn't be the same. That her life experiences led her here, to me, and that we wouldn't be where we are without what happened hanging over the years it took to get here. I don't speak about how the things she went through are what shaped her into my little demon, and that I'm not sure I could love her if she were any other way.

I tell her what she wants to hear.

"And I'd burn the fucking world down if it meant I could go back and do things differently."

She sniffs as a lone tear trails down her cheek. Silently, she steps forward, reaching around to push the lighter into my hand. "Prove it."

Confusion flickers across my face, but she doesn't see it as she turns and walks away. "Misty!" I call after her retreating form.

She leaves without another word, the click of the door shutting behind her reverberating throughout my apartment as she leaves me alone to figure out how to escape this mess.

Even if I break the chair, the rope is too tight, and I'm too tall to get my hands in front of me.

Closing my eyes, I breathe deep through my nose as I flip the top of the lighter open, careful not to drop it. My teeth clench together so tightly I swear I hear a molar crack as I anticipate the pain to come.

Sweat beads at my forehead, rolling down to mix with the blood smeared at my temple. The searing heat rips a cry from my throat when the flame licks my raw skin. I struggle not to scream out loud, focusing all my pain and rage on the woman who's made my heart swell so extensively that I fear it may burst from my chest.

And I let the rope burn.

Misty

Luca is a fool for showing me where he lives.

Tonight, il mio mostro will meet his end.

And I along with him.

But I don't fear Death.

No. I look forward to him claiming me as his own.

"Don't be a fool this time. Don't let him get into your head with his flowery words and saccharine lies," Adam's apparition spits out, lounging on Luca's sofa as though he were real.

I'm having a psychotic break.

And I welcome it, knowing it will make tonight easier to get through.

The lights are dim as I crouch near the refrigerator, readying my syringe for the moment Luca walks through the door. There's a vase of roses on the kitchen island that wasn't there two weeks ago—the last time I saw him. Their edges are dark and curled, dead petals littering the sparkling granite. Next to it, a vanilla candle has been burned nearly down to the bottom of its holder.

"How fitting. He got you dead flowers, and you're both about to die," Adam singsongs in a way he never would have when he was alive.

"Shut up," I snap. "When I make it to Hell, you better run and hide."

"Don't be so touchy." He appears next to me, reaching out to knock his knuckles against my temple. I swear my hair flutters around the indentation of his wrist.

The sound of keys jingling outside the door cuts off my reply. My heart jumps in my chest, swelling with anticipation as Luca lets himself in and tosses his keys into the bowl on the table in the small entryway. His footsteps are heavy as he comes further into the apartment, pausing just inside the kitchen.

Looking up, I hold my breath, watching him inhale heavily through his nose. A smirk pulls at his lips as he looks around, eyes darkening as he reaches for the dial on the wall to turn the lights up so he can hunt for his prey.

"Where are you, piccola demone?" he calls out into the space.

As he picks up a foot to begin searching for me, I strike like a viper, stabbing my needle into his thigh and injecting him with enough Mizoladam to put him out for at least a good thirty minutes. He jerks back with a howl of pained surprise before reaching down to grab my hair.

Tossing the needle aside, I spring to my feet, using the momentum of him pulling me up to pounce. Luca's anger radiates through his touch, his grip tight enough that I swear I hear the hair rip from my scalp. The pain spurs me on as I wrap my legs around his waist, my skirt bunching around my upper thighs as I tangle my hands in his dark strands. "Take me to bed," I demand before smashing my lips against his.

"Stop being a whore and carve him up already." Adam stands behind us, retracing every step Luca takes into his bedroom.

I do my best to ignore him, focusing instead on Luca's hiss of pain as I untwist my fingers from his silky strands to grab his wrists. He pulls back abruptly, flinging me off him to land on the plush mattress before stepping back and shaking the pain off his hands, a string of curses flying from his lips as he walks a circle around the room.

His chest heaves with anger, and I prop myself up on my elbows, wondering how much longer it will take before the drowsiness kicks in. I pushed the limit with the sedative. It shouldn't take long, but with Luca's size, I'm also not sure how long it will last. I'm hoping for at least a half hour, but as he stalks back toward me, his muscles rippling beneath the tight fabric of his black shirt, I'm reminded of how huge he is.

"Where have you been?" he demands, reaching for my ankle to pull me to the edge of the bed. His wrists are still raw and red but don't look nearly as bad as I expected them to. I knew the rope would take a while to burn through, and that his skin was already scratched raw from him trying to escape, but a flicker of disappointment squeezes my chest as I realize I didn't do as much damage as I'd hoped.

Shrugging, I peer up at him from beneath my thick lashes, legs falling open as he crawls between them and settles his weight over me, pushing me into the mattress with his sheer size. "I've been around."

"Around," he repeats, the word thickly layered with sarcasm. Luca sits up, straddling my waist as he grabs ahold of my shirt and rips it in two, flinging both pieces of the thin material to the ground. "I've been looking for you everywhere!" he fumes.

His face contorts with fury, making him look like an absolute lunatic. Once upon a time, he might have been the stuff of my nightmares.

Now, he's my every waking fantasy.

His large hands grip my waist, and before I can say a word, he rises on his knees and flips me onto my stomach. The straps of my bra bite into my skin as he tears at them, destroying the garment in under two seconds as he pulls it from my body. "You got what you wanted, piccola demone. Now it's time for me to get what I want."

"And what's that, il mio mostro?" My words come out strangled as he fists my hair and pulls my head back, stretching my neck taut.

His other hand comes around to pinch one of my nipples, rolling it between his fingers roughly as he begins to laugh. The sensation, paired with his voice, sends a thrilling streak of pleasure straight between my legs.

But it's short-lived as he leans down to whisper in my ear, his words clipped, the edges of sleep creeping into his voice. "You. No…more…revenge. Just you."

That pleasure hightails it to my chest and pierces through my heart.

"Don't fall for it, sis." Adam sits on the edge of the bed as Luca releases me and rolls to his side.

"How much…did you give…me?" he whispers.

Not giving a shit about my being half-naked, I rise and begin to move him into a position that will provide me with better access to his body. "Enough to get what we want from you."

"We?" The word tapers off as Luca finally falls asleep.

As I run my fingers lightly over his face and think

about how beautiful he looks, Adam lets out a dramatic sigh beside me. *"Fucking finally. Get to work, Mari."*

Reluctantly, I tear myself away from Luca's side to retrieve the bag I brought with me. Knives, saws, little bottles of acid, and different sizes of pliers clink together as I toss the black leather bag onto the bed.

"You know, I can get your pound of flesh without killing him," I whisper to my brother, who glares down at Luca's sleeping form like his very being is a stain on this earth.

And I suppose to Adam, he is.

"Now, where would the fun in that be?" His eyes lift to mine, our twin blue-green gazes locking as we size each other up. *"What happened to you, Mari? You used to live for this. Killing him fueled your will to live. Is his cock really so magical that once you got a taste of it, it made you stupid? Did he fuck the sense out of your brain?"* He knocks his knuckles against my temple.

Smacking his hand away, I gnash my teeth at him, letting out a feral cry of frustration.

My brother is right. This has to be done.

I dig into the bag, careful not to break the acid bottles as I fish out my Spyderco Ladybug. Flipping the blade up, I sink it into Luca's thigh, just above the knee—before I lose the nerve.

Adam's laughter fills the air, and he begins to clap. *"There she is!"*

His praise spurs me on as I quickly and efficiently begin to slice pieces of Luca's flesh from his body like you'd scrape the top off a stick of butter. I'm careful not to go too deep. I don't want him bleeding out before he wakes.

And through it all, il mio mostro sleeps peacefully, unaware of the nightmare he'll awake to.

Time moves slowly as I create art with my blade—carving my real name with precision and the word *mine* over Luca's heart—but with every piece of skin I take, Adam grows more frustrated that I don't land a killing blow.

No matter how many times I've retrieved a longer blade and sat upon Luca's chest to spear it through his heart, I simply cannot bring myself to end his life this way.

"You're a fucking coward!" Adam slaps his hand on the bed, rattling the plethora of blades that span the left side of the mattress. *"Just fucking do it already!"*

"I can't!" I scream back, flinging my hands out to the side and sending Luca's blood splattering over his crisp, white sheets.

Well, they *were* white. Now they're mottled with red.

"I swear to God, Mari, just kill him! Avenge me!" Adam roars into my ear, his spittle spraying over the side of my face as tears line my eyes.

A tremor rocks through Luca's body.

My time is up.

"You stupid fucking bitch," Adam spits out. *"So this is where your loyalty lies, huh? With the man that murdered me in cold blood?"*

Thrashing my head back and forth, I drop the knife and press my hands to my temples, smearing Luca's blood over my skin as I close my eyes tightly. "He didn't murder you!"

"He's lying! Of course, he's going to say that! He just wants to keep fucking you. You're both sadistic fucks."

"Misty?" Luca whispers my name. His eyes flutter open, his chest beginning to rise and fall more rapidly as he groans in pain. "Misty, what have you done?"

"Nothing. She had all this time to kill you, and she did nothing!"

"I'm sorry. I can't do it. I can't do it. Please don't make me do it," I repeat over and over as Luca comes to, more aware with every passing second.

"Misty?" he reprises my name gently, despite the pain he must be feeling. "Who are you talking to?"

Luca

Coming out from under sedation is like living a fever dream. Your hearing intensifies—sometimes your taste if you had something shoved down your throat to help you breathe. You feel everything that was done to you, and you struggle to open your eyes to make sense of where you are.

To make sense of what happened while you were vulnerable to the doctors and nurses—or, in my case, a crazy little demon who's out for my blood.

And there's a lot of it—blood, that is.

Every single part of me feels like it's on fire as I peer down at the mess Misty made. There are parts of me where she flayed my flesh, and the blood has dried. It cracks as I shift, pouring new red rivers from the wounds.

Misty's name—her *real* name, Marisela—is a

bloody mess over my right pec, and the word *mine* is jaggedly carved over my left—directly over my heart.

"Misty, what have you done?" I question, choosing to continue using the name she picked because of me. She's covered in crimson, still half-naked from earlier, grasping at her head while repeating how sorry she is and that she can't do it.

Her beautiful eyes dart to the left, and she gnashes her teeth at the air as I ask her, "Misty, who are you talking to?"

My head pounds, temples throbbing as my adrenaline spikes. Shifting, I do my best to prop myself higher on my pillow. Every slight motion rips a fresh wave of discomfort from me as my eyes begin to focus better.

She's mumbling to herself, kneeling at my side with a long blade lying by her knees and pieces of my skin scattered all around us. Her craftsmanship is magnificent, ensuring I suffer while not bleeding out.

The pain is severe, and I fight hard to swallow the bile that rises in my throat.

Tears line her eyes as she looks at me. "I have to do it. I have to do it for Adam."

She reaches for the knife, prompting another burst of adrenaline to course through my veins and mask the pain. Moving quickly, I snatch her wrist and haul her up my body, letting out a pained grunt as she lands on my chest. "Then let me savor your sweet cunt once more before you send me to Hell."

I'm naked, my clothes a tattered mess all around us, and despite the distress my body is in, my cock still hardens at the sight of her covered in me. Her tits are bare, painted with thick red, and my words make her pussy wet, the arousal seeping from between her legs to mingle with the blood smeared over my chest.

As quick as a snap, her demeanor changes. "Even near death, my pussy is what you're thinking about? Then I guess I've done my job, il mio mostro."

Her lips smash against mine for a brief moment before she climbs the rest of my body, pulling her skirt higher until her warm, wet center is positioned over my face. "I'd make you beg for your last meal, but I feel generous."

My blood on her tits cracks and flakes off as she reaches for a knife, slicing through the fabric of her skirt and tossing the garment and blade to the side. I close my mouth around her. She's sweet and tangy as I slide my tongue through her slit before plunging through her folds, twisting her nipples and pulling as she rides my face.

A different kind of heat pours through me. This one is all liquid fire as it runs through my veins and straight to my engorged cock. If this is to be my end, I gladly accept it.

But I'm taking her down with me.

Misty tips her head back, hands reaching behind her to grasp my cock, giving it a few tugs before she lifts onto her knees and spins around to seat herself on my face. She mutters, "Shut up, Adam." But the words die on her lips as she deep-throats my length, pulling a groan from my throat that vibrates up into her core.

Pain and pleasure mesh in a bloody, slippery dance as she sucks my cock and I eat her pussy like we're teenagers trying to fit everything in before curfew. Her little mewls and gasps every time I suck her clit spur me on, and when her teeth graze the sensitive skin of my cock, I roughly slap her ass in return before pulling apart her cheeks, giving me easier access to nibble on her swollen bud.

"Ahh!" she cries out around me, trying to pull her head back, but I wrap my thighs around her neck and hold her down, bucking my hips into her face as I reach for the knife at our side.

As I tense them to keep her hostage, I map all the places she cut me, leaving more raw flesh than regular skin. If I hadn't woken up when I did, I wonder if she would have kept going until I looked like one of those images of the human body and the muscular system.

Her garbled noises cause her throat to constrict around my cock, pulling my release from me. The sounds of her gagging fill me with delight, and I wait until she's thrashing around, desperately trying to escape, until I let her go.

Misty scrambles to the end of the bed, her back to me, as she gasps for air and spits my cum from between her lips while cursing my name.

And the satisfaction is nothing compared to the howl she lets out as I rise and sink the long blade into her side.

Before she can get away, I pull her backward by her hips, sinking into her with one thrust, my pelvis meeting her backside as I bottom out inside her. "Did you think you'd be the only one to draw blood tonight, piccola demone?"

She claws at the knife in her side, debating whether to pull it out or not, as I fuck her into the mattress. A high-pitched squeal fills the air as I continue to drill into her, watching as her blood streams around the knife and mixes with mine on the sheets. "Harder!" she moans before snarling, "I said shut the fuck up, Adam!"

"He isn't here! I am!" I fuck her roughly, demanding that her body recognizes who it belongs to. Reminding her that every second between us is real and that whatever she's hallucinating isn't. "Everything of yours belongs to me, Misty. Do you understand?" I lean forward, pulling her head back by her hair, and whisper, "Including that fucked up mind. So if I hear you say his name one more time, I will cut out that perfect tongue."

"Fuck you!" she spits, slamming her hips back against me, the blade in her side forgotten.

Chuckling, I twist her strands around my knuckles again, pulling her head back at what must be a painful angle. "Oh, I am, baby. Can you feel me?" I reach out with my other hand, pressing on her lower abdomen with every ardent thrust. "Can you feel me here?"

What leaves her lips isn't an answer, more of a strangled cry as her pussy convulses around me. "What about here?" I ask, sliding my hand to the knife and twisting it before pulling it out.

She screams, bolting forward and spinning to shove me back. I expect it, allowing her to push me against the pillows and helping her as she climbs on top of me and seats herself on my cock again. Blood spills from her body, streaming down her side in a beautiful waterfall as she curls her lip. "And what about you, Luca? Can *you* feel *me*?"

A flash of silver catches my eye too late, glinting off the moonlight that pours through my bedroom window as it slashes across the space between us.

Right into my abdomen before she turns it upward to sink beneath my rib cage.

Luca stares up at me. The look on his face is not exactly one of surprise but of shock, all the same. We both pause, staring at each other for one second. Then two. Three. Four. Five.

Then, he somehow manages to knock me back with a roar, spearing into me with his rock-hard cock like he's going to split me in half with it.

His blood is everywhere, spilling onto me as he rips the knife from his body and flings it across the room. And still, Luca fucks me like a man possessed. A man who feels no pain, only the immeasurable pleasure that cascades between our bodies.

"That's it, punish me, il mio mostro." I laugh up into his face, smearing his blood over my body like I want it to seep into my skin. Luca watches in awe as I mix our essences together—blood and sweat and cum—all coming together to form another layer of *us*.

His jaw tics, teeth grinding together as I gather his crimson liquid and bathe my breasts in it, painting my nipples until they're shining with his life substance. The wound in my side throbs dully with every thrust, and when Luca's hips shudder, I know he must be getting lightheaded from the blood loss.

He reaches up, wiping his hand over the red liquid that stains his chest before slapping my clit with the same hand. Adjusting his weight on his knees, he rubs my clit with a bloody thumb as his cock slows, dragging against my inner walls, trying to coax one more orgasm from me before we leave this world.

"Come for me, Marisela." The use of my real name has me falling apart beneath him, tears lining my eyes as I claw at his arms while stars dance across my vision.

Something warm fills me. At the same time, a searing coolness sinks into my chest. I look down as pain blossoms beneath my rib cage to see that he's grabbed another knife from where they lie scattered at the edge of the bed, and stabbed me.

A mirror image of the lethal blow I inflicted upon him.

Then Luca falls back with a quiet groan.

Slowly, I manage to crawl up his side, curling into him as we both bleed out.

"I wish you'd confronted me sooner," he whispers, wrapping an arm around me.

Something moves out of the corner of my eye. *"Finally. I was beginning to think you didn't love me anymore, dear sister."*

I don't grace the apparition of my dead brother with a response. Instead, I tilt my head and prop my chin on the hand resting over my name that's etched into his skin. "We will have more time. We just have to get to the afterlife first."

"We won't be headed to the same place, piccolo demone." His words are quiet, warped by the blood beginning to bubble in his throat.

"Do you think I won't follow you into the pits of Hell, il mio mostro? I plan on holding you over the flames for the rest of our intertwined eternity. My own personal spit-roasted monster. Ready for me to take a bite whenever I want." I smile up at him, lifting a hand to push his silky dark hair out of his eyes.

"Is that what awaits us then? An endless cycle of tormenting each other? Fucking and fighting, forever bathed in flames? It doesn't sound so bad to me. The Devil will probably separate us, though. Hell is supposed to be a punishment. What awaits us sounds like Heaven." He returns my smile, something shining in the depths of his bronze eyes that I've been waiting years to see.

"I dare the Devil to try and separate us. I'll always find you. Your damnation is mine, and mine alone."

"My own personal Angel of Death." His body shudders before settling into a state of eerie stillness.

"Can you feel it? The end?" I try to keep the concern from dripping into my questions.

My body grows numb; whatever pain I might have felt is taken over by the stony weight of sheer desperation as I cling to what's left of my life long enough to see Luca through his death.

"I'm cold. That's all I feel. That, and your heart. It's slowing down. Matching the beat of mine." He pulls his gaze from mine, glassy eyes finding the ceiling.

"Just another sign that this is how it's meant to be. Don't worry about the cold. I'll keep you warm."

"I think… I think it's coming. Do you promise to find me?" He threads his fingers through mine, his other hand tightening on my shoulder.

"I told you, Luca, I'll always find you. Nothing can keep me away." My chest swells painfully with utter devotion—a disciple saying goodbye to her God.

The light leaves his eyes. Bronze fading into nothing but a dull brown.

Even in death, Luca is still the most beautiful thing I've ever seen.

"I love you." My whispered sentiment reaches ears that can't hear the words. But somehow, I know he knew without me saying anything out loud.

And in the end, I think he finally loved me, too.

In the end, we were the perfect match: a monster and his demon.

A cough sputters in my throat. Blood flies from between my lips, metallic and sweet, spraying Luca's face with specks of red.

"I'll see you soon, il mio mostro. I'll see y—"

Epilogue

LUCA

ell is nothing like I expected.

No evil presence greets me, no dancing little minions with pitchforks to herd me into the fiery bowels of the underworld. No three-headed dog or river that needs to be crossed.

Instead, there's glittering chandeliers and familiar cinnamon furniture. There's an oval bar and heavy dark doors that lead to halls I remember walking a million times. But instead of being filled with masked strangers, Désirer is empty.

Silent.

Lonely.

Desperation crushes my chest at the thought of being stuck here for an eternity. Out of all the punishments I imagined waiting for me, this is the last thing I would have thought of.

I move to the bar, grab a bottle of whiskey from the top shelf, and pour a glass before pausing. Leaving the full glass on the bar top, I lift the bottle to my lips and gulp down the sweet amber liquid, welcoming the burn that settles in my stomach like an old friend.

A familiar scent—vanilla and roses—floats into the room on a warm breeze.

"Is the liquor sweeter down here, il mio mostro?"

The bottle slips from my grasp as I meet my piccola demone's beautiful gaze. "You came."

Her full lips curve upward as she makes her way toward me, hips swaying as she prowls slowly. Her body is perfect, not a scratch marring her skin, encased in a short, white, feathery nightdress. A pair of angel wings grace her back, held up by straps that encircle her shoulders—the silvery platinum ones she never wore at Désirer.

Misty reaches for the bottle that fell but never broke, reappearing on the bar top as though I'd never dropped it in the first place. She lifts it to her lips and grins, saying, "I told you I'd find you."

"And I told you, this seems more like Heaven than Hell." I keep my gaze trained on her as I walk out from behind the bar.

She takes a sip and shrugs before placing the bottle back on the smooth wooden surface. "Maybe the Devil owed me a favor."

"Or maybe this is part of my punishment, and you're not really here." My hand tingles as I reach for her, anticipating the flesh to dissolve or melt beneath my touch.

I don't realize I've stopped breathing until my palm finds her waist, warm and supple as I splay my fingers over the soft feathered material of her dress.

My lungs fill with a sharp gasp as her tinkling giggle fills the room. Her hands slide up my arms, leaving goosebumps in their wake as she hooks them behind my neck. "I'm real, Luca. This is real."

I willingly bend as she pulls me down for a kiss, meeting her lips with ardent fervor. I rip at her dress, the feathers flying everywhere, surrounding us in a soft, downy white cloud.

She's real.

She's real, and she's here, and she's mine.

She's *mine*.

"Mine," I growl against her lips in case the Devil himself is listening.

"Mine," she repeats with the same warning as we dare Death to try and separate us. "Now fuck me, Luca."

"Patience, piccola demone," I whisper against her lips, even as I lift her petite body and sink into her wet heat. "We have time, and I plan on spending every second of it filling you so full that you'll be dripping with me for the rest of eternity."

Her cries of satisfaction cut off her laughter, and later—when we find that the glass can indeed break and cause a type of pain that washes away instantly—cries of pleasured pain join in.

Our symphony of forever.

Hers and mine.

And Death's.

Return
to where
it all began.

Flip the page for the
first two chapters of
Jackson and Ginny's story,
Burn With Me.

GINNY

Age 10

I've always hated my appearance.

Deep copper hair. Sky blue eyes. Ivory skin with a distinct dusting of freckles across my nose and cheeks.

People have always looked.

No one has ever made me feel the way Christopher Calloway is making me feel right now.

Like I'm dog poo on the bottom of his shoe that he just stepped on when he came inside his house and found his parents with the social worker and me. As if it was *my* fault his parents signed up to be foster parents. *My* fault my mother died last night after losing her battle with cancer, and now I need to be placed somewhere.

The rage on his face is poorly concealed, but his

parents and Mrs. Trech aren't paying attention to him. His eyes flit up to his mother as he pushes off the wall before making his way over to me. Gripping my backpack tightly, I try to make myself smaller as he comes closer until he's towering over me. He glances back at his parents once more before looking me over with his lip curled in distaste.

"I don't want you here," he says between clenched teeth, voice low so his parents won't hear him.

Shrugging slightly, I peek up at him and respond, "I don't want to be here."

Letting out a soft snort, he reaches out and grabs a lock of my hair, tugging it hard enough to make me wince. "Don't fuck with me."

His words are lost on me. From what I've gathered in the short amount of time I've been in the Calloway's home, I've learned that Mr. Calloway is a very successful surgeon, and Mrs. Calloway stays at home. Christopher is four years older than I am and is their pride and joy. But Mrs. Calloway has always wanted a daughter, and I suspect Christopher isn't too happy about having to share his parents' attention.

"If you try anything, I'll make your life a living hell," Christopher sneers quietly, just before his parents and Mrs. Trech appear behind him.

"Christopher, are you welcoming Guinevere to

our home? We're so sorry to hear about your mother, dear. Come, I'll show you to your new room." Mrs. Calloway holds her hand out for me to take as her son beams up at her like he's the poster boy for the welcoming committee.

Fighting the urge to roll my eyes, I don't take the offered hand but take a step closer to her to show her I'm ready to go.

I can feel Christopher's eyes burning a hole into my back as I walk away.

Age 12

There are shadows outside my bedroom door.

Ones I've come to expect at least once a week.

They belong to Christopher and will remain there for a few minutes before he pushes the door open softly, so it doesn't creak and alert his parents.

My chest tightens as I pull the blankets beneath my chin and turn toward the wall, pretending to be asleep.

Just like I always do when he comes in late at night.

There's a scratch in the pink wallpaper. I stare at it, letting my mind wander to anywhere other than here, as I hear the soft sounds of his footsteps while he crosses the room.

"Ginny? You awake?" His voice is soft and quiet.

Sometimes, I think he knows I am, but it's easier for us both to pretend I'm not.

My mind roams to other places. Happier places. Places where my imaginary friend shows up and distracts me from Christopher's shallow breaths and the wet sound of skin on skin as he touches himself.

Christopher's view of me went from angry and annoyed, to angry and obsessed in the first year I lived with the Calloways. He was always picking on me, pinching my skin, or tugging my hair. And I dare not say anything because, as far as foster homes went, I had won the golden ticket. What was dealing with a bit of bullying?

But then, as we got older, his friends started to notice me. They'd make comments about my appearance, like boys their age do, and all of a sudden, Christopher's attention turned from bullying to possessive.

A few months ago, he started coming to my room, asking if I was awake. I've always pretended to be asleep, and sometimes I wonder what he would do if I met him with a wide-eyed stare and said, "Yes, I'm awake. Why are you in my bedroom?"

So, I started to make up places in my mind. And since I didn't really have any friends, I made up one of those, too. My imaginary friend is a boy because I think it's easier to cope that way. He's taller than me, with golden brown eyes, milk chocolate hair, and an English accent.

When he visits me, I can imagine I'm somewhere far away. In another part of the world where what's happening to me can't happen there.

Sometimes, we'll play on a playground or run through the sand on a beach. Once, we went on an Arctic expedition and played with some penguins. But for all the months I've been imagining him, I've never given him a name. And he's never offered me one.

He's just…my stranger.

Age 14

"God, your sister is fucking hot, dude," Richard Barnes says as he openly stares at me from where he and Chris are throwing a football back and forth in the pool.

It's the end of summer, and the sun is scorching. Mr. and Mrs. Calloway are hosting a pool party barbeque, so I'm in a bathing suit, reading a book in a chair as I dry off from a swim.

"She's not my fucking sister. Don't call her that," Chris snaps back at him before turning his dark eyes to my figure.

I'm wearing sunglasses, so they can't tell that I'm

watching them. But somehow, I think Chris knows anyway.

"If you don't think of her as a sister, then why'd you tell the whole football team that if anyone goes near her next year, you'll kill them? Screams big bro energy to me, dude."

Hearing what Richard says doesn't surprise me in the slightest. It isn't because he thinks of me as a little sister. It's because he thinks of me as *his*.

Every night, his shadow shows up at my door, and I curl in on myself, wondering if it will be the night he finally takes what he thinks belongs to him. He's about to head off to New York for his first year of college in a few days, and he's warned off every boy in school from ever pursuing me romantically.

Everyone thinks he's just being a protective big brother.

But big brothers aren't supposed to put their hands on you.

They aren't supposed to sneak into your room and peel off your blanket. Touch you over your clothes while they touch themselves. I stopped pretending to be asleep a long time ago once he told me he knew I was awake.

All I do is stare at a spot on the ceiling and imagine that it's my stranger touching me instead. Because no matter how unwelcome Chris' touch is, my body reacts to it, so he thinks I like it. It's confusing for us both, I guess. He's started to say dirty things while he touches me. Things that make my body feel tingly all over. I don't like it. But it makes my body feel good.

I'm ashamed of it.

It's disgusting, and wrong, and I *hate* him for it.

But his parents treat me like I'm their own even though they won't adopt me because Chris asked them not to.

Because in his fucked up brain, he thinks if they do, it will solidify that what he's doing is wrong. That as long as we don't share a last name, it validates his actions.

Chris sends me a look that tells me to expect his presence tonight. "None of those fuckwads even know what to do with their dicks. The last thing my parents need is a teenage pregnancy scandal. They don't need to take care of another stray."

His words send ire through my veins. I clench my teeth and flip a page to make it look like I'm not paying attention.

Tonight, this *stray* is going to bite back.

I'm sitting on my bed when Chris walks in around midnight. My bedside lamp is on, casting a glow over the room as I read, and I look up to see him freeze for a moment before silently shutting the door behind him.

"What are you doing?" he asks.

"What are *you* doing?" I challenge, turning my attention back to my book.

Powerful would be the way to describe how I feel right now, but when I glance at him, that feeling turns to lead in my stomach. His lips turn up in a grin as he runs a hand through his dark hair and continues to walk closer to my bed.

Swallowing, I place my bookmark in the book and set it on my nightstand before swinging my legs over the side of the bed and fixing him with a mean glare. "Go away, Chris."

Faster than I can blink, he knocks me back, covering my mouth with one hand while the other holds my wrists. He's straddling my waist, and as I start to struggle, I can feel that it's making him hard.

"Do you think just because I'm leaving for school, that means you're going to be rid of me, Ginny?" He leans down so that his lips rest against my ear. "Maybe I should give you something to think about until I come back at winter break."

His hips press into mine, and tears prick my eyes as he starts to rub against me. Shouting against his hand, I begin to thrash my body against his, trying to throw him off me, but he's much stronger than I am.

Chris laughs as his hips keep rolling against me, his penis rubbing between my legs and causing a sensation that I fight against with every fiber of my being.

"Just fucking lay there and take it, Gin. Too bad you're not old enough for me to fuck yet. Or I'd ruin your hairy snatch before I leave," he grunts into my ear.

He's careful not to go too fast so the bed doesn't squeak. And his hand is pressed so hard over my mouth and nose that I struggle to breathe. His other hand grips my wrists so tightly that I'm sure there will be bruises I'll have to hide.

Shutting my eyes tightly, I imagine a different body above me. A different boy whose name I don't know and whose face is always blurry in my mind. A gentler touch–more experienced. The pressure between my legs grows, and with each passing second, the line blurs between what I know shouldn't feel good and what does.

Maybe this will be the last straw, and I'll finally tell Chris' parents what he's been doing to me for the last two and a half years.

Chris buries his face in my hair and grunts as his hips start to slow. The ache between my legs dies as he pushes up off of me and looks down at my face. For a split second, he looks alarmed. Tears are streaming down my cheeks, and the straps to my night camisole have slipped down my shaking shoulders. My pajama pants have a wet spot on them that matches the one on his gray sweats, and I almost open my mouth to scream.

But I don't.

Because soon he'll be gone, and I'll be free.

Age 17

For the first time since I stepped foot into the Calloway home, I'm witnessing Chris try desperately not to cry.

Tears line his eyes as he grips my jaw roughly, though not hard enough to leave bruises. His other hand wraps around my neck, forehead pressed hard against mine, pushing me into the wall as I claw at his hands.

"You fucking *bitch*. You stupid fucking bitch. How could you do this to me?!"

His breath reeks of alcohol. It's winter break of my senior year, and Chris' parents are out of town because his dad has a conference to attend in Boston. I didn't think Chris would come back this year because he hasn't spent much time at home since he left for college.

Ever since that night in my room three years ago, he hasn't touched me or touched himself in front of me. Part of me has always wondered what made him stop, but I never wanted to dwell on it. The fact that he stopped was all that mattered.

Imagine my surprise when he walked in the door five minutes ago. Drunk and very much *not* supposed to be here.

He'd distanced himself from us–typical college boy behavior, according to his mother. Whatever the reason, I was glad for it. It took some time, but I started to come out of my shell with him gone.

I have friends now. Kids at school have stopped thinking of me as his weird little foster sister. The boys have started to pay attention to me.

And suddenly, it hits me why Chris is so angry.

"It was supposed to be *mine*, Guinevere. *MINE!* And you went and gave it away like a dumb fucking whore!"

"Stop it! You're hurting me! Let go of me, Chris!" My voice is shrill as my nails scratch at his flesh. But it doesn't even phase him.

"How'd you let him do it, huh? Did you let him fuck you in the back seat of his truck? Or did he bring you to his house when his parents weren't home and take his time with you in his bed?"

His grip tightens, and I whimper in pain, digging my nails into his hands. The air in my throat is cut off, blood rushing to my head as I struggle to breathe.

"Did you let him fuck you in the ass like a dirty little slut? Was it worth it? Did he make it good for you?" He slurs his words as he nuzzles my neck before speaking against my cheek. "Because you'll never know what it's like to be fucked again. Do you hear me? I am going to make sure no one ever so much as *thinks* they can fuck you. And if you think I'm going to touch your filthy, tainted cunt now, you're wrong. So tell me, was it worth it?"

Pushing off me, he drops his hands away from my body, and I crumple to the ground, gasping for air. One hand braces my weight on the floor as the other reaches up to gingerly touch my neck. My eyes raise, and I watch him from beneath my lashes as he paces the length of my bedroom, gripping his hair tightly.

"FUUUUUCK!" he shouts, causing me to jump.

Seconds later, his fingers tangle in my hair, yanking my head back as he shouts in my face, "Did you think I wouldn't find out?!"

Find out that I gave my virginity to Timmy Rhodes. A sweet boy who doesn't have a lot of friends and who I don't find attractive. A boy who stumbled his way through the act and didn't mind that my eyes were closed the whole time as I imagined that it was *my stranger* I was giving my innocence away to.

So that Chris couldn't steal the only shred of it I had left.

"Let go of me!" My watery screams match his as I

wonder how I let it get this far. There's something sick and twisted in his mind, and any other foster home would have been better than letting this depraved man in front of me think he *owns* me.

His tears dry up as he looks down at me, and his lips twist in a grin. "You know, I probably would have lost interest once I fucked you."

His hands pull my hair harder, contorting my neck at an uncomfortable angle. "Now? Now, I'm going to make your life a living hell, just like I promised I would when you walked into this house seven years ago. You're a sickness, Ginny. A sickness that only *I* can cure. But now? Now, I'm going to enjoy watching you rot."

A cry escapes my lips as he tosses me away from him like a rag doll. A toy he's done playing with. All I can think of as I watch him walk out of my room and slam the door is how I can't wait to graduate and get as far away from him as I fucking can.

Age 18

"A full ride?" My mouth drops in awe as Mr. and Mrs. Calloway beam at me from across the kitchen table.

"Of course, dear girl. And with Christopher starting med school, he'll barely be home. It only makes sense that you two live together. No rent. We'll still send a check every month to help out with utilities and groceries. You won't have to worry about a thing," Christine says with her full lips parted in a smile, her chestnut hair perfectly coiffed.

Panic grips me at the thought of living with Chris full-time with no one else around. Briefly, I wonder what would happen if I open my mouth and tell the Calloways what their son has been doing to me all these years. But the thought of breaking Christine and Calvin's hearts is too much. Their son is *everything* to them. He's the perfect all-American football star I've never seen be aggressive toward anyone other than me. He's always worn his mask well and fooled anyone he's ever wanted.

Except me.

And if there is one thing I've learned from him that I'm thankful for, it's how to fool people into thinking you're something you're not.

So, I'll put on a show for the Calloways, and I'll make all three of them think I'm going along with their little plan. Part of me feels terrible for using their money, but I'll get a good education. I'll keep myself busy so I don't even have to be home with Chris. Then, once I've graduated, I'll get as far away as possible.

My eyes glitter, and my lips turn up in the best

genuine smile I can feign. "That's so generous of you guys. Thank you so much. I promise I won't let you down."

Jackson

"**S**uck *harder*."

Fuck. What does a guy have to do to get a woman in this city to suck his cock like she's a fucking Hoover vacuum?

The woman on her knees, I don't even remember her name, looks up at me with annoyance painted on her overly dressed up face. It makes me smirk as I slap her cheek lightly. "What's wrong, sweetheart? Thought you were gonna get fucked slow and sweet and that I'd let you stay the night?"

She pulls back off my cock and wipes at her mouth roughly as she gets to her feet. "You're a fucking asshole."

"Not news. And *you* signed an NDA, so if a word of this gets out, I'll make sure you're doing this as a job for the rest of your life. And you *won't* be getting paid." My phone vibrates on the coffee table in front of me, and I tuck myself back into my slacks before leaning forward to grab it.

The woman makes a high-pitched huffing noise as she gathers her stuff and makes her way across the hardwood floor of my living room. "It isn't news that you're an arrogant playboy, but I didn't think you were the type to leave a woman unsatisfied."

She's baiting me, and I'm not stupid enough to open my mouth and bite the hook she's dangling like she's trying to catch a big, fat, billion-dollar fish. Ignoring her, I open my phone and groan when I see it's a text from my uncle.

The meeting tonight isn't optional.

There's a *ding* that signals the elevator has taken the desperate female out of my penthouse, and I glance behind me to make sure she's actually gone before letting my head fall back on the couch. Part of me feels slightly bad about how I treated her. But every woman I've brought home lately is the fucking same. They pretend like they know what they're doing and then try to act demure, as if somehow going slow and acting shy is going to do the trick for me.

Slow and shy has never been my thing. I don't want an inexperienced virgin, or a woman pretending to be one. I want a woman to ride my dick like she's trying to split herself in half with it. Hard, raw, and primal is what gets me going. Graze my cock with your teeth. Tell me to fuck you harder. My idea of a good time is breaking a fucking bed frame.

And sure, there have been plenty of women who have left me satisfied sexually, but they don't keep my interest beyond that. They think that alone earns them a right to be on my arm. A right to the title of *girlfriend*, eventually leading to *fiancée*, then *wife*.

Men in my position shouldn't have wives. Or girlfriends, for that matter. It always ends messy. So why even bother? Love doesn't exist for men like me— men of power with billions at their fingertips and the world at their feet. We're greedy bastards, and one woman will never be enough.

If that were really true, you wouldn't feel the way you do, you lonely prick.

Regardless, this life has grown dull. I'm bored with the same routine over and over. No one ever says *no*. No one ever *challenges* me.

My phone buzzes again.

In fact, I want you there early.

Checking my watch, I realize that if I'm gonna be early, I need to leave now. I don't even know what this stupid meeting my uncle wants me at is about.

Or why it has to be at some restaurant he partially owns instead of at the office where they usually are.

"Fucking stupid. Like I don't have better things to do on a Friday night." Standing, I pull my shirt over my head and head upstairs to my bedroom. The intense floral perfume of the woman is clinging to my skin, and I need to wash it away if I plan on bringing someone else home tonight.

The word Decadence beams down at me in neon cursive as Robert pulls my black town car up to the curb. I've never been here, or even heard my uncle talk about it, but as soon as I step through the doors, I can see why he insisted on meeting here.

It's dimly lit, but I've always thought that makes a woman more attractive. And attractive is definitely the word I'd use to describe the waitresses.

"How can I help you today?" A pretty brunette beams up at me from the hostess stand—a blush already staining her full cheeks as she does her best to maintain eye contact.

"That depends. What time do you get off work, gorgeous?" The way her whole face flushes, I'll bet she just creamed herself.

Before she can answer, a stunning dark-haired

woman wearing a cream-colored pantsuit appears behind her with an unapproving glare like an overprotective mother. "That won't be necessary, Jackson. Your uncle is in the back. You can follow me."

"And you are?"

"My name is Carmela." Her tone makes me think she doesn't like me, and I wonder what she has to do with the meeting and how she knows anything about me to begin with.

Carmela saunters through the tables, pausing to say hello to a few patrons, while I check out the waitresses and try to decide which one I'll let finish the job the no-name woman from earlier walked out on.

As far as restaurants go, this is a nice one. Exposed brick, distressed wood, bronze furnishings—for the area, it's not exactly upscale, but it's better than Serafina's. A flash of rust catches my eye, and I turn my gaze.

It's been a long time since a woman took my breath away. But this one, there's something about this one that's special. Dark copper hair that curls down below her breasts, bright blue eyes that are piercing—even in the dim lighting. Full, bubble-gum pink lips.

She throws her head back and laughs at something a customer says before nodding and moving away from the table she's at. Distantly, I hear my name behind me, but I've already turned and started walking toward the ginger goddess.

If I have to guess, I'd say she's about five-six. Her back is to me as she types something into the computer system, but she doesn't startle when I give her my smoothest, "Hi, there."

Looking over her shoulder, she doesn't appear phased at all as she gives me a once-over and turns back around. "Can I help you with something?"

Her tone is ice cold, and my eyebrows knit together in disbelief. Women don't ever respond to me like this. Affronted, I scoff, "What's your name?"

Sighing, she spins around and locks eyes with me like I'm a rodent she just caught sneaking into the kitchen. "Scarlett. And you are?"

Scarlett. Appropriate.

Now that I'm closer, I can see she has freckles over her cheeks and nose. They make her seem endearing. Innocent. The one thing that I *don't* want in a woman.

But her fiery attitude tells me that even if she's innocent, she's got some bite to her.

Sticking my hand out for her to shake, I flash my best *fuck me* smile and respond, "Jackson Tailor."

Her contemptuous look drops, lips opening in surprise, as her eyes widen a fraction. A rosy hue breaks out on the apples of her cheeks, and she's about to say something when I hear my uncle speak behind me.

"Jackson, leave Ginny alone and let her do her job."

My eyebrow raises as I smirk at her before mouthing *'Ginny.'* She glares at me before her eyes snap to my uncle as he walks up and places himself between us.

"Shit, I'm sorry. I'm still getting used to the name tag thing," he tells her quietly.

The way her eyes soften and warm when she looks at him doesn't sit right with me. She's gotta be in her mid-twenties, at least. My uncle may be a good-looking man for his age, but he's *ancient* compared to her.

"It's okay, Mr. Tailor. Don't worry about it. Can I get you anything?" Her tone is hopeful and doting, and it makes my stomach roil.

"Are you trying to get one up on Aunt Sadie? Fooling around with a younger woman because she went and married her little boyfriend already?" It's a low blow, but I'm irrationally angry that the old man obviously got to the little gingersnap before I could.

Only a year has passed since he signed the divorce papers my aunt gave him. He had the perfect woman. If there is such a thing, my Aunt Sadie is it. And instead of treasuring her like a dragon with its gold, he fucked around on her publicly and drove her into the arms of a man that's twenty years younger than her.

"That's enough, Jackson," he warns.

Ginny's face is crimson as she furiously shakes her head. "It isn't like that!"

Uncle Scott jerks his chin in the direction behind me and says, "Let's go."

Pushing around me, he heads to the other side of the restaurant, where there's a long hall, but I don't follow him. Instead, I step closer to Ginny, lowering my head and asking, "What's it like, then? Because that look you were giving him was definitely a little too eager, if you ask me."

"You're disgusting. He's my boss, and older than my father. Not my style," she grits out as she glares up at me. She's gripping the pen she's holding so tightly that it might snap at any moment.

"What *is* your style? I'd love to find out." Taking another step toward her, I smirk as she takes one back, yet the fight never leaves her narrowed eyes.

"Not *you*. That's for damn sure." She straightens her spine, attempting to make herself look taller.

"I'm a man of many talents, *Scarlett*. Why don't you give me a chance to show you?" Reaching out for a lock of her hair, my hand freezes mid-air when she flinches. It's minimal, as if she catches herself and steels her body against it, but her breathing has picked up, and her eyes are wide as she looks at me. Hardened, as if she's bracing herself for impact.

Who hurt you, my fiery little ember?

Dropping my hand, I step back and stick my hands in my pockets. "Okay, I'm sorry. I'm not usually this much of a dick. You caught me on a bad night. Why don't you join me for a drink when you're off work? I'll make it up to you."

She searches my face silently for any sign of insincerity before her posture relaxes, and she lets out a long breath. Shaking her head, she reaches up and tucks her hair behind one ear. "I don't think so. I have to get back to work." Then she turns and walks into the open-concept kitchen.

Watching until she disappears, I slowly turn and follow my uncle to where he's impatiently waiting outside a bronze-finished door. When I reach him, I extend my hand. "I'm sorry, that was uncalled for."

He smacks it away, then lightly hits me upside the head. "You're damn right it was. And you embarrassed the poor girl. You better apologize."

"I did! And I asked if she wants to get a drink after work so I can apologize again."

"With *words*, you jackass! Not with your dick!"

Well, he's got me there.

CHECK OUT THE OTHER
BOOKS IN THE ANGELS OF
DÉSIRER SERIES

BURN WITH ME
LIE WITH ME
PLAY WITH ME

AVAILABLE ON KINDLE UNLIMITED
AND WHEREVER BOOKS ARE SOLD

Afterword

As sad as I am that this series has ended, Misty and Luca were the perfect goodbye.

Writing their story really fucked with my head a little, but I kind of liked it.

I had no intention of writing their story yet, if ever, but after a beta said I couldn't leave Play With Me the way I did, I decided to sit down to see if I could at least get down bones to wrap up the Angels of Désirer, and the words for this book ended up pouring out of me.

All good things must come to an end, but this won't be the last time we see these characters—well, it's the last time we'll see Misty and Luca but not the rest of the Désirer crew.

Stay tuned.

Acknowledgments

I want to give a special thanks to my entire alpha/beta team for reading this.

It was a lot of fuckery.

I appreciate you.

I want to give a special thanks to Rachel McEwan for my cover. The entire series looks amazing together, and you are brilliant!

And to my editor, Virginia Carey, who is always down for whatever I throw at her, no matter how fucked up it is.

Also, a very special thanks to April because without your feedback, Misty and Luca wouldn't have gotten their story.

About the Author

D.L. Darby lives in Anchorage, Alaska, with her husband and two fur babies.

By day, she's a hairstylist, and by night, she's continuously drafting new ideas on her "murder board" at home. While she writes across multiple romance sub-genres, you can always expect to find spicy alpha males and strong-willed women with a flair for dramatics in her stories.

Where the Flowers Bloom

Sugar and Scotch Duet

Slice of Temptation

Sweet as Sin

Weekend Wonderland Duet

Peppermint Wishes

Starry Night Kisses

Angels of Désirer Series

Burn With Me

Lie With Me

Play With Me

Die With Me

Serial Killer Book Club

Dolls & Daggers

Sirens & Stilettos

Devious Desires

Devious Temptation